Billy
the
Blue-Stitched
Baseball

JOHN W. SCAFETTA

PAGE PUBLISHING, INC.
Conneaut Lake, PA

First originally published by Page Publishing 2021

ISBN 978-1-6624-4582-8 (pbk)
ISBN 978-1-6624-6831-5 (hc)
ISBN 978-1-6624-4583-5 (digital)

Printed in the United States of America

For Sarah, Sienna Grace, and Grandpa Bill.

The new season was brimming full
of hope and bright lights.
The grass freshly mowed and the baselines snow-white.
Louisville sluggers were slathered with brown tar,
Anxiously awaiting hard hits from all-stars.

The fielders, on guard, stood stoutly in position.
From the look on their faces, they knew their mission.
The crack of the bat made a beautiful sound,
As the pitcher hurdled home from the base of the mound.

Billy had seen it before and was full of pure wonder,
At the roar of the crowd growing louder than thunder.
He watched the beautiful game with
the others in the shade.
As each waited their turn, the spheres they'd play.

But one thing troubled young Billy,
the sprightly young ball.
There was something on the outside
that made him feel small.
See, one thing about Billy you probably should know,
Before he dreamt big dreams of making
it to the top of the show.

At the factory long ago, soon after he was born,
A simple mistake was made that most others would mourn.
A hapless old worker way late for his bed,
Forgot standard baseball stitches should be laced up in red.

Instead, the careless crafter fastened
the young ball with blue.
But Billy didn't mind; in the mirror, he was shiny and new.
Years passed, and his passion for the game rapidly grew.
For early in life, Billy was blessed with a giant park view.

Grandpa and Billy watched games from near and afar.

Talking home runs, base hits, and

mounting trips to the snack bar.

He found escape in the game and

soon forgot the blue stitches.

He chose fun over fear as he watched all the pitches.

From there, his dream formed as quickly as a spark.

But as he grew older, others left him in the dark.

Some older baseballs would laugh and cruelly say,

"Billy the Blue-Stitched Baseball, you're

not getting in the game today."

"Your laces are strange. Your stitches are wrong!
You'll never get picked for this game.
You just don't belong!"
But Billy was bound and determined;
he had such a kind heart.
With his love for the game, the other
baseballs couldn't tear him apart.

Billy cheered all of his friends as they circled the yard.
He would not give in; the blue-stitched
kid firmly kept his guard.
Long ago, Grandpa once told him,
"Stand tall with a big smile.
One day, young Billy, you'll be hit a country mile!"

Life is not simply all about fame and big dreams.
It's much better to do right and be part of the team.
For Billy knew baseball was simply a game.
If he focused on the jokes, it would be a great shame.

So Billy took Grandpa's advice and smiled large and wide.
With the sun shining bright, there was no reason to hide.
The call up to the show one day would soon come.
And the pitch would be beautiful with a magical hum.

The bat would connect on each unique blue lace,
And the joy in his heart would match the smile on his face.
He remembered Grandpa, who would long ago say,
"Baseball is wonderful and all, but it's only a game!"

"Have fun with it all, no matter your troubles.
Respect the other baseballs, and your
happiness will turn to doubles.
You'll win some games and lose others at times.
But if you show up with a smile, the
biggest hills you'll climb!"

Billy kept thinking good thoughts and continued upbeat.

It was just at that moment the coach said, "Take a seat!"

A new pitcher was up; he had gotten the call.

So the hurler dug in the bucket to grab a shiny new ball.

To Billy's surprise and the shock of the team,
The hopeful blue-stitched baseball
had just caught his dream.
It was Billy's turn now as the batter dug in.
On the very first pitch, the hitter did grin.

He swung with all his might.
He swung for great heights.
Well over the centerfield wall,
Went Billy the Blue-Stitched Baseball!

He rolled down the hill as the crowd went crazy.

His feelings ran wild; his thoughts were all hazy.

At the bottom of the hill lay Billy's best friend.

With a tear in his eye, there's no better end.

Billy beamed from ear to ear with so much delight.
For his Grandpa knew all along Billy
had played the game right.

The End

About the Author

John W. Scafetta is an author and longtime sportswriter. As a New York native who has been immersed in baseball since birth, Scafetta has written in the sports pages of the *Rochester Democrat and Chronicle*, the *Las Vegas Review-Journal*, and the *Orange County Register*. He lives in Atlanta, Georgia, with his wife and young daughter. *Billy the Blue-Stitched Baseball* is his first children's book.

CPSIA information can be obtained
at www.ICGtesting.com
Printed in the USA
BVHW022314250821
614931BV00006B/7

9 781662 468315